MADELINE

SAYS MERCI

MADELINE
SAYS MERCI
THE ALWAYS-BE-POLITE BOOK

Based on
the characters
created by

**LUDWIG
BEMELMANS**

JOHN BEMELMANS MARCIANO

to all the children

who gladly give up their seats

VIKING
Published by the Penguin Group
Penguin Putnam Books for Young Readers, 345 Hudson Street,
New York, New York 10014, U.S.A.
Penguin Books Ltd, Registered Offices:
Harmondsworth, Middlesex, England
First published in 2001 by Viking, a division of Penguin Putnam
Books for Young Readers.
1 2 3 4 5 6 7 8 9 10

Library of Congress Cataloging-in-Publication Data
Marciano, John Bemelmans.
Madeline says merci : the always be polite book / by John
Bemelmans Marciano.
p. cm.
ISBN 0-670-03505-X
1. Etiquette for children and teenagers—Juvenile literature. I.
Title. BJ1857.C5 M312 2001   395.1'22—dc21
2001001781
Printed in Hong Kong
Set in Bodoni Book
Designed by Angela Carlino
The illustrations for this book were rendered in pencil and gouache.

In an old house in Paris
That was covered with vines
Lived twelve little girls
In two straight lines.

Day in, day out,
They got along fine;
They'd hardly ever
Shout or whine.

To each other they were polite

Except for the occasional pillow fight.

The pages that follow offer advice
On how to be polite and nice.
As you read, please keep in mind
It all comes down to being kind.
Don't forget to think of others—
Parents, pets, and little brothers.

hello

The proper way to greet
Someone you chance to meet

Is to look them in the eye
And say "Hello" or even "Hi."

The hello that's most worthwhile
Is the one delivered with a . . .

smile!

When a grown-up is introduced to you
Look up and say, "How do you do?"
If they extend their hand to take
Offer back a nice firm shake.

But when you meet the queen for tea
The proper thing is to curtsy.

To greet a dog, you kneel down low
And give a gentle pat hello.

When meeting a group, don't just say "Hey."
Say "Hello" to each, and to all the same way.

But when the most you can do is wave your hand
The other person will understand.

& thank you

To ask for something, what do you say?
"Please," or in Paris, *"S'il vous plaît."*

When it's your turn to pass the plate
Smile, be generous, don't hesitate.

Now that you have what you desired,

The words
thank
you
are what's required.

"You're welcome" is the thing to say
After thanks have come your way.

Every gift deserves appreciation
No matter what the situation:

If it's something
you asked for

A happy surprise
from the store

Unwanted gifts
you find a bore

What you had
seven of before.

A thank you spoken
Is a very nice token

But a thank you letter
Is even better

Because getting a thank you in the mail
Will brighten your day, without fail.

kindness

& consideration

If someone wants to talk to you
Listen to them until they're through.
No matter if they talk till dawn,
Don't interrupt, look bored, or yawn.
Hold your words and don't be vexed;
Your turn to speak is coming next.

Interrupt *only* if you see
A prisoner running free,
A porcupine who wants to play,
A solar eclipse (look away!),
A bucking, snorting runaway horse,
Or a house on fire, of course.

Don't be selfish and given to greed:

"Here, I have more than I need."

It can be lots of fun to share

And taking turns is always fair.

Don't punch and shove when you play.
Only a Bad Hat acts that way.

Nobody likes a boastful bore
Who brags, "My dad's a rich ambassador!"

And to whisper, point, and stare
Shows you're rude beyond compare.

An animal is a friend, not a toy;

This sort of thing she does not enjoy.

Sometimes she wants to be left alone
To sleep or chew her favorite bone.

If you let her have her way
She'll come to you when she wants to play.

No one minds a little help.
Start by cleaning up after yourself.
Do the dishes, sweep the floor,
Take out the garbage, hold the door.

sorry

Accidents happen without intent or warning:
Madeline spilled her juice this morning.

"Excuse me, please, I beg your pardon,"
And after that it was forgotten.

If you do something you know is wrong
Such as going where you don't belong

Don't make it worse by telling lies;
Say you're sorry and apologize.

Teasing someone isn't cool—
It's never funny, often cruel.

To remedy this ugly business
Try and beg for some forgiveness.

If you do what you shouldn't dare
And give your teacher quite a scare,

Apologize to her and then
Never do that thing again.

Excuse me!

Sorry!

Pardon me!

Does not mean that you are free
To push or shove obnoxiously.

Being sorry's most
Important part
Is that it comes
Straight from the heart.

good
night

"Good-bye" lets other people know
That you are sad to see them go.

Now it is time to go to bed
There's nothing more that needs be said,
Except the words "Sleep well, good night,"
Which let you know that all is right.

So Miss Clavel, please turn out the light
On this book of how to be polite.

FINIS